Hannah Safferman is studying to become an elementary school teacher. She lives in Michigan with an extremely supportive family and two dogs. Her goal in life is to spread awareness of differences and disabilities in people so that everyone is seen as a valued individual.

Hannah Safferman

IT'S OK TO BE ANXIOUS

AUSTIN MACAULEY PUBLISHERS™

LONDON • CAMBRIDGE • NEW YORK • SHARJAH

Copyright © Hannah Safferman (2018)

Ordering Information:
Quantity sales: special discounts are available on quantity purchases by corporations, associations, and others. For details, contact the publisher at the address below.

Safferman, Hannah
It's OK to be Anxious

ISBN 9781641826266 (Paperback)
ISBN 9781641826273 (Hardback)
ISBN 9781641826280 (E-Book)

The main category of the book — Self-help and personal development

www.austinmacauley.com/us

First Published (2018)
Austin Macauley Publishers LLC
40 Wall Street, 28th Floor
New York, NY 10005
USA

mail-usa@austinmacauley.com
+1 (646) 5125767

I would like to acknowledge Katherine Budrick for inspiring and supporting me in writing a book.

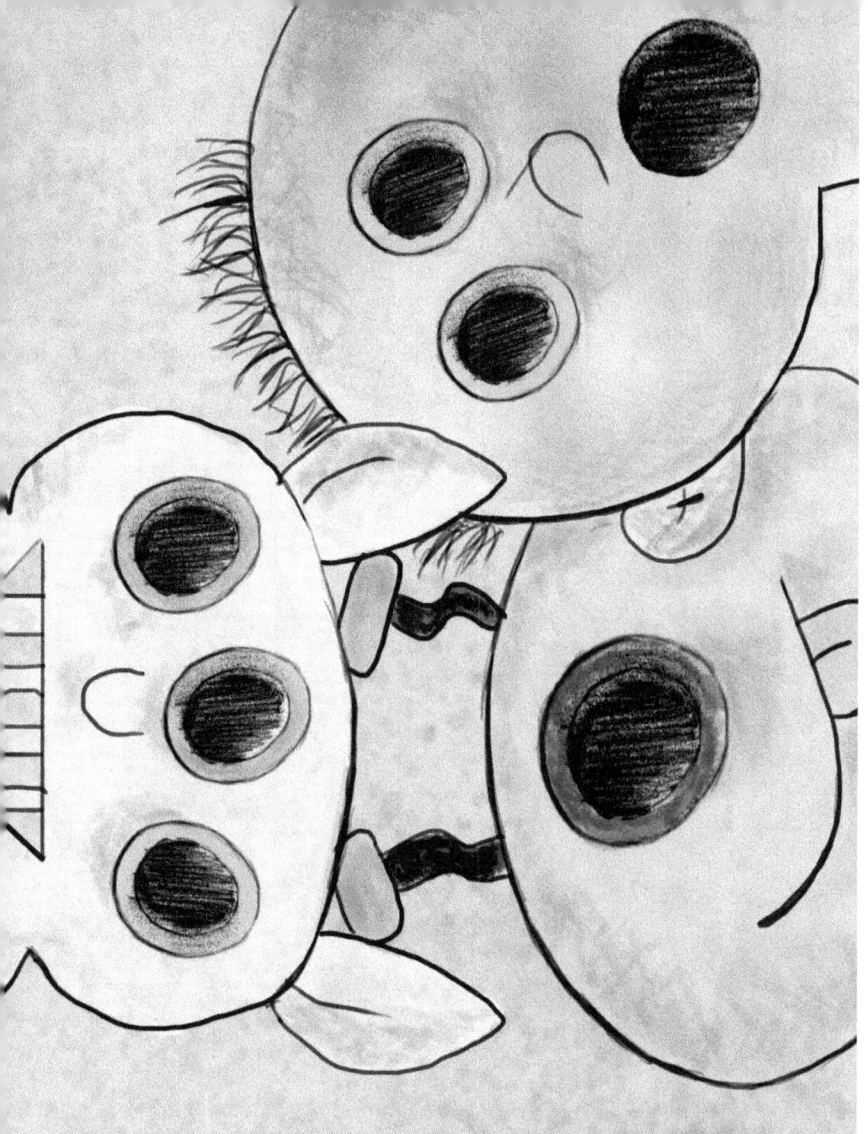

You can feel a certain way after something scary or surprising happens.

Sometimes, you wake up in the middle of the night from having a bad dream.

You may get nervous before a big test, game, or recital.

Sometimes, parts of your body hurt or you
cannot control something.

When these things happen, you may feel anxious. This is an emotion that may not feel very pleasant.

You may be thinking of a lot of different things at once or feeling lots of different emotions. It may feel like there is a race car, zooming around in your head.

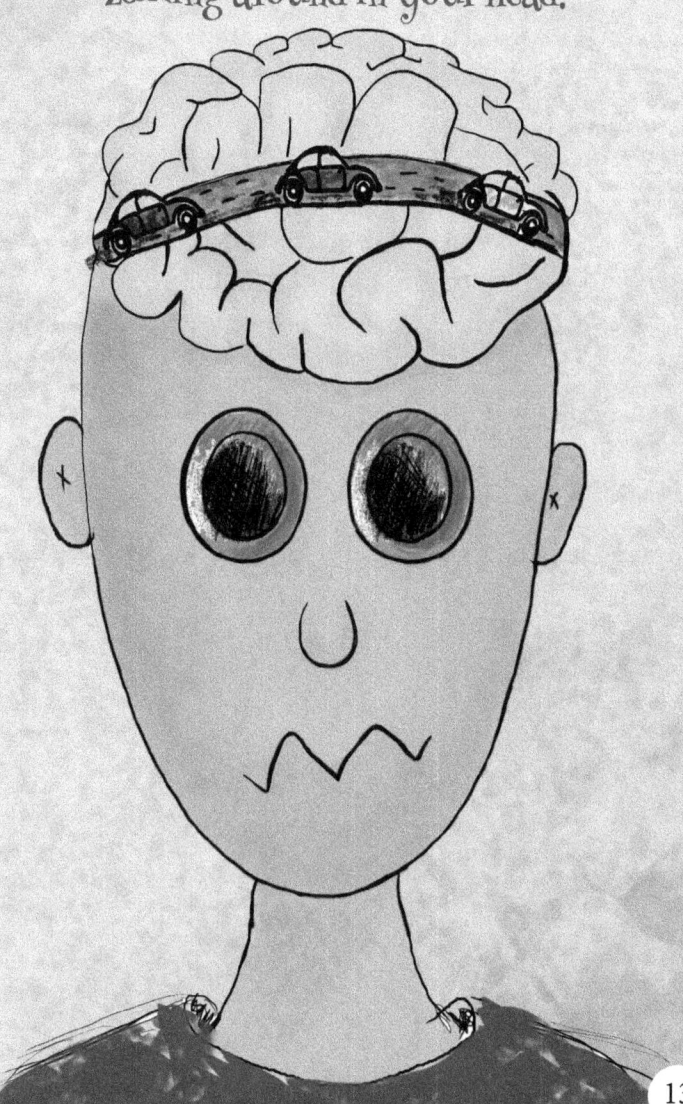

Your tummy may feel funny like it is
doing back flips on the monkey bars.
You may get annoyed with family,
teachers, and friends, and may not want
to play with them or you may want them
to help you feel better.

It's ok to feel this way and there are ways to
feel better when you are anxious.
You can take snake breaths. This is when
you breathe in deep and fill up your belly
then breathe out while making a snake sound.

Sssssssss.

Try taking small sips of water, milk, or juice.

You can squeeze your hands together into a tight ball or you can make a fist with one hand at a time.

Going on a walk with people who love you can also help the anxiety go away. Remember, feeling different emotions is important and completely normal. Emotions can help keep you safe and healthy.

What makes you feel anxious?
What can you do when you feel anxious?